STAR WARS

EWOKS JOIN THE FIGHT

WRITTEN BY MICHAEL SIGLAIN

ART BY PILOT STUDIO

Disney • LUCASFILM

PRESS

Los Angeles • New York

Printed in the United States of America

First Edition, August 2015

FAC-029261-15303

Library of Congress Control Number on file

ISBN 978-1-4847-0548-3

High above a forest moon
was the Empire's secret weapon.
The secret weapon was
a new Death Star.

The rebels sent
Han, Luke, Leia, and Chewie
on a mission to the forest moon.

The rebels had to find a bunker.

Inside the bunker was a machine.

The machine kept the Death Star safe.

The rebels had to destroy the machine.

The rebels searched for the bunker.
The rebels saw two biker scouts.
The biker scouts patrolled the forest.
They also guarded the bunker.

Han and Chewie had to stop
the biker scouts.
They did not want the
biker scouts to warn the Empire.

The biker scouts escaped.
Luke and Leia jumped on
speeder bikes.

They chased the biker scouts.

Luke and Leia split up.

Luke used his lightsaber.

Luke stopped one biker scout.

Then he returned to the rebels.

Leia stopped the other
biker scout.
But their fight broke her speeder.
Leia was lost in the forest.

A small creature approached Leia.
It was an Ewok.
Ewoks are small and furry.
They live in the forest.

Leia gave the Ewok some food.
Then a hidden biker scout attacked.
The Ewok helped Leia stop the scout.

Leia and the Ewok were now friends.
The Ewok took Leia to his village.

Han, Luke, and Chewie searched
the forest for Leia.
They took R2-D2 and C-3PO
with them.

In the forest was a trap.

The rebels walked into the trap.

The rebels were stuck in a net.

R2-D2 cut them down.

The rebels landed on the ground.
They saw the Ewoks.
The Ewoks had set the trap.

The Ewoks tied up the rebels.
The Ewoks took the rebels
to their village.

Then Leia appeared.
She told the Ewoks that the rebels
were her friends.
The Ewoks did not listen to her.

Luke knew what to do.
He knew that the Ewoks could
help them.
Luke used the Force.

Luke made C-3PO float
through the air.

The Ewoks were scared.
They thought C-3PO
had special powers.
The Ewoks freed the rebels.

The rebels learned that Chief Chirpa was the leader of the Ewoks. And the Ewok who had helped Leia was named Wicket.

C-3PO told the Ewoks
all about the rebels.
The Ewoks liked the rebels.
They did not like the
biker scouts.

The Ewoks agreed to help
the rebels.
The rebels were now
a part of the tribe.

The Ewoks took the rebels
to the hidden bunker.
The rebels surprised the
biker scouts.

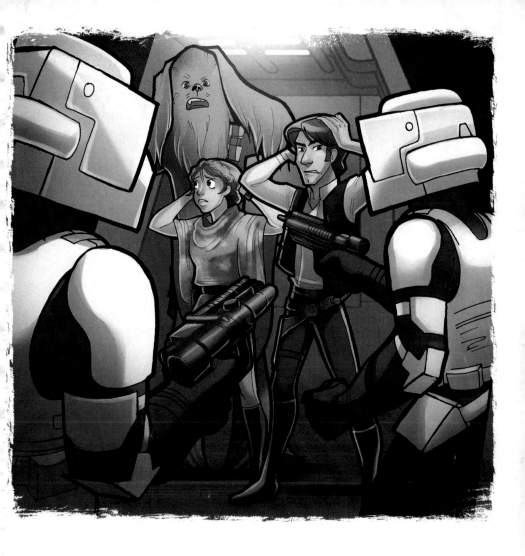

But inside the bunker were
more biker scouts.
They were waiting for
the rebels.

The rebels had been captured.
It was time for the Ewoks
to join the fight!

There was a big battle.
The Ewoks helped the rebels.

The Ewoks and the rebels
fought hard.
They stopped the biker scouts.
They destroyed the bunker.

The rebels destroyed the
new Death Star.
The rebels and the Ewoks
saved the day!